Teddy Bear's
FIRST
WORD BOOK

A NOTE TO PARENTS:

As parents, we can play a vital role in helping our children to read by practising with them at home. Sitting and working together in a relaxed manner will give you the chance to support and encourage your child to read, and show that you value reading and language work.

TEDDY BEAR'S FIRST WORD BOOK makes the ideal starting point for young readers. You can best help your child to understand the new words by going through the book alphabetically with him or her. Encourage your child to look at each picture and then describe it to you. Don't worry if your child does not immediately guess a word – go on to another and come back to it later. Remember, never do too much at any one time. Above all, make sure you give your child lots of encouragement, support and praise. The most important thing for a child to realize is that reading is good, enjoyable fun!.

This edition first published in 1988
by Gallery Books
An imprint of W.H. Smith Publishers Inc.
112 Madison Avenue
New York, New York 10016

By arrangement with Octopus Books Limited

Copyright © 1988 Octopus Books Limited

ISBN 0 8317 8667 1

Printed in Hungary

Teddy Bear's FIRST WORD BOOK

ABC

Illustrated by
Paul Stickland

GALLERY BOOKS
An Imprint of W. H. Smith Publishers Inc.
112 Madison Avenue
New York City 10016

Aa Bb

Ff Gg Hh

Ll Mm

Cc Dd Ee

Ii Jj Kk

Nn

Oo Pp

Rr Ss

Ww Xx

Qq

Tt Uu Vv

Yy Zz

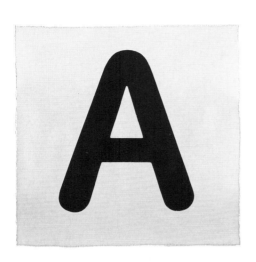 

A a

apple

ant

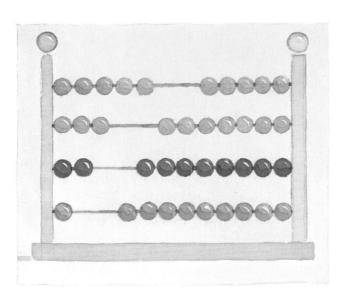 

abacus

anchor

acrobat

arrow

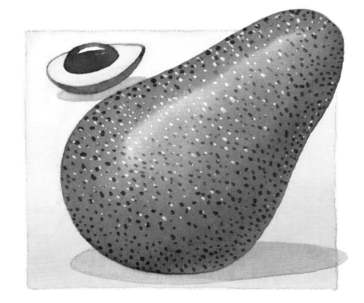

avocado

alligator

B b

boat

book

bed

bicycle

balloon

butterfly

beetle

bubble

C C

castle

cake

cow

carrot

camel

cactus

camera

computer

canoe

D 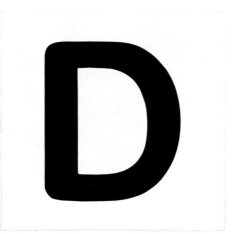 d

dolphin

door

donkey

dog

dinosaur

duck

daisy

E e

elephant

engine

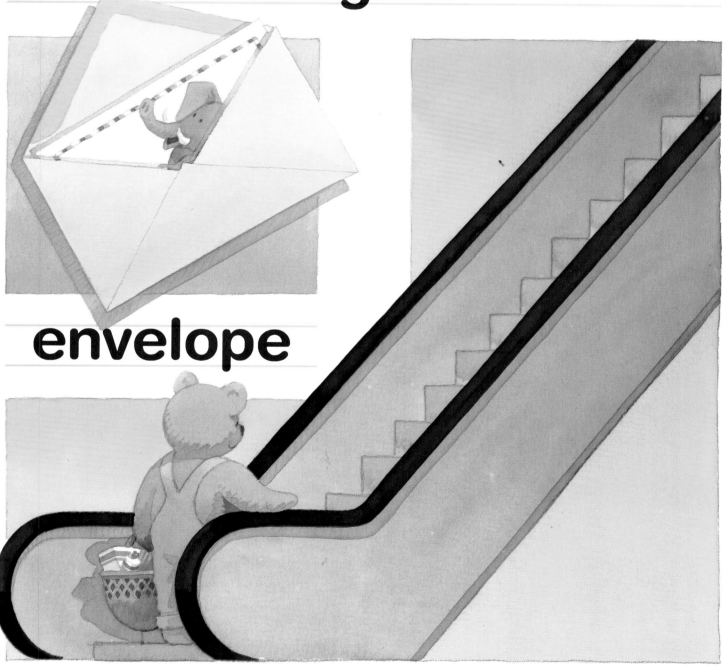

envelope

escalator

fish   fork

firework

feather

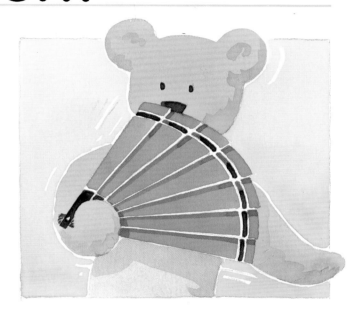

fan

fence

 G  g

goggles

gate

guitar

go-cart

gorilla

goat

garage

H h

hamburger **horse**

hammock

helicopter

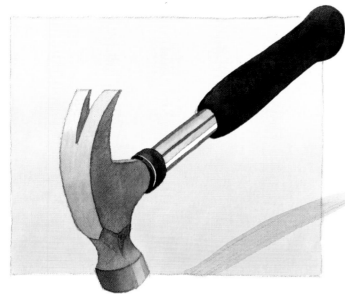

hammer

hen

hippopotamus

I i

igloo

iguana

ink

invitation

J j

jigsaw

juggler

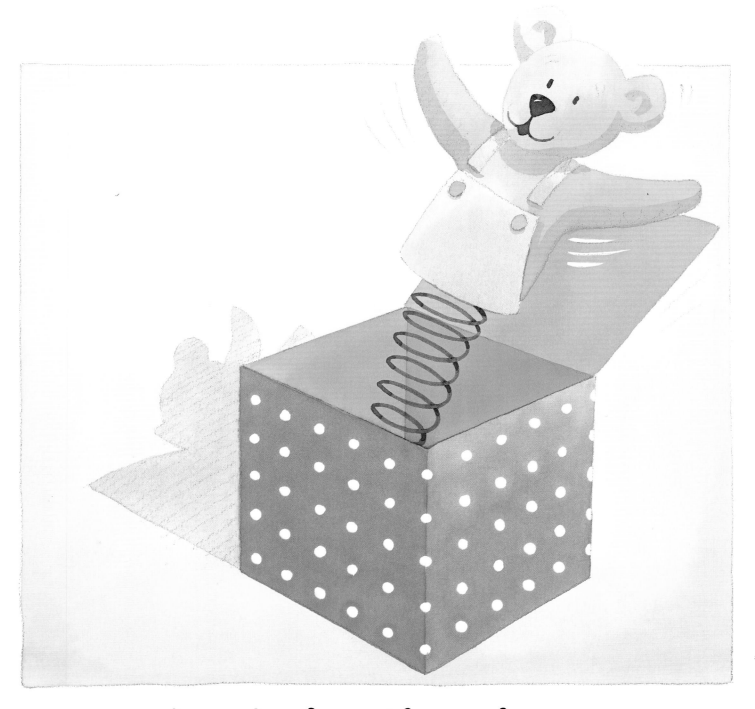

jack-in-the-box

jacket

jug

K k

kennel

kite

kettle

kitten

kangaroo　　　**king**

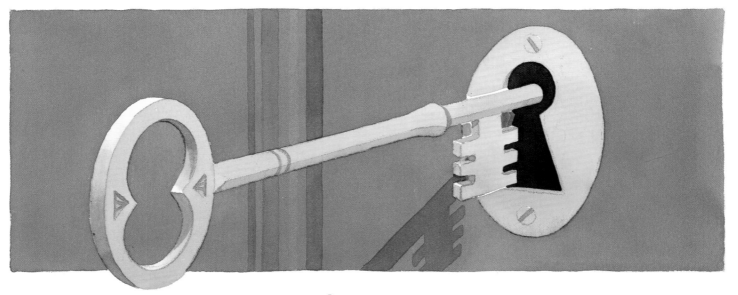

key

L l

lasso

ladder

lamb

ladybug

lion

lighthouse

M m

mirror

milk shake

mushroom

mouse

medal

mug

monkey

motorbike

N

n

net

noodles

newspaper

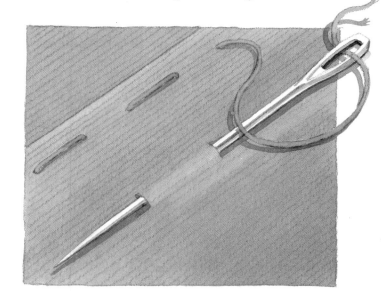

needle

nest

necklace

nail

O o

octopus

orange

ostrich

ox

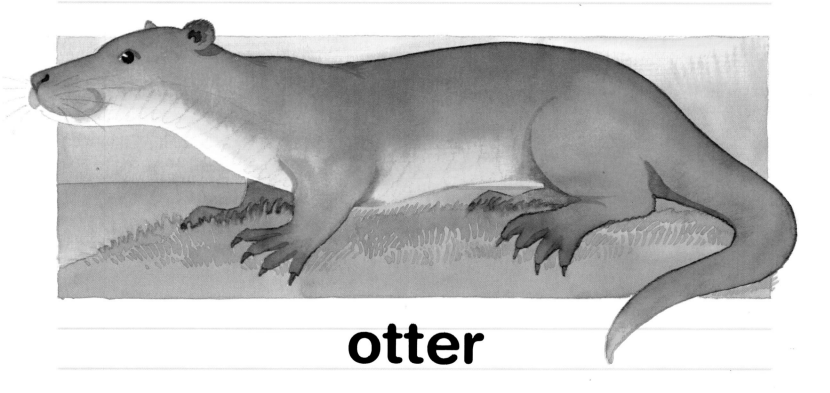

otter

P p

paintbox

parachute

pajamas

panda

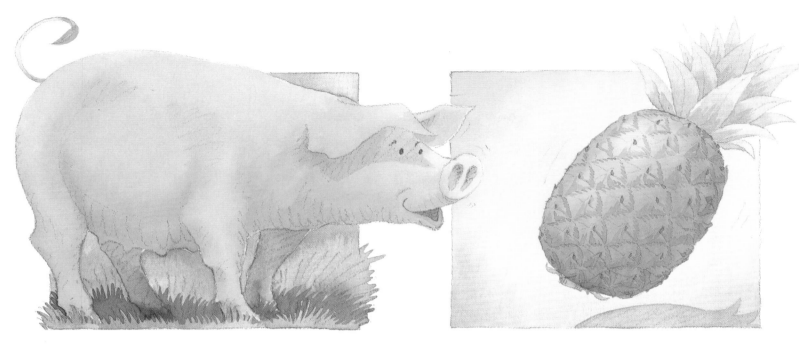

pig

pineapple

piano

penguin

pie

parrot

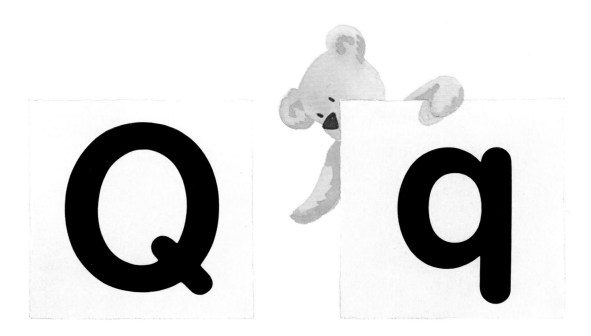

queen

quilt

R r

rabbit

robot

raincoat

rainbow

rose

radio

rocket

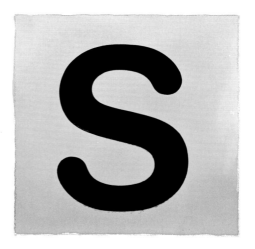 

S s

socks

sandwich

sand castle

seesaw

seal

sunflower

submarine

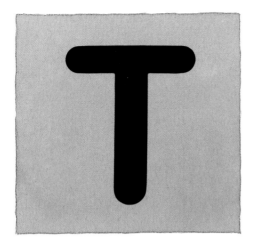 

tent

towel

table

teapot

tiger

tee shirt

television

tortoise

tomato

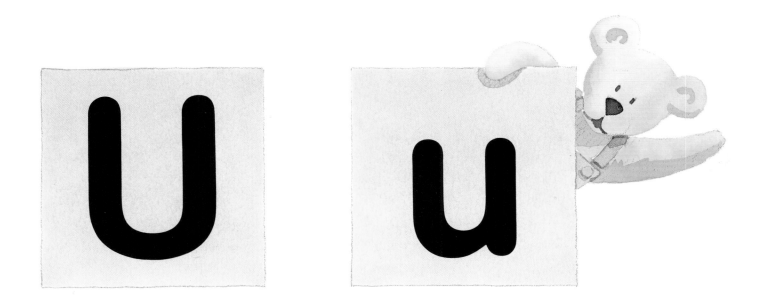

umbrella

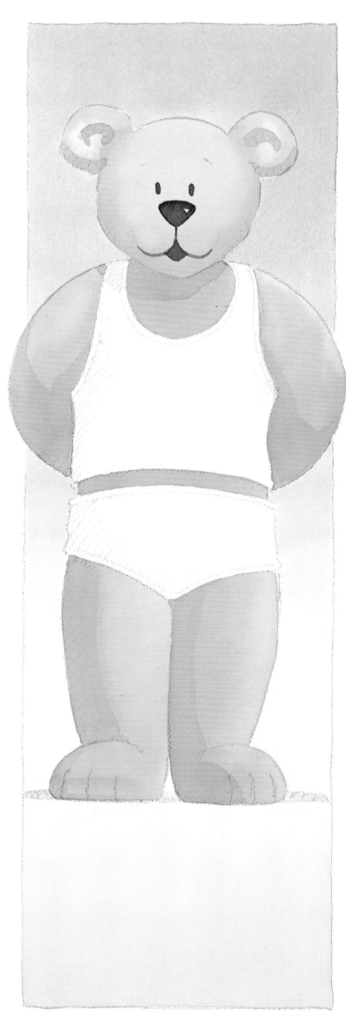

upstairs

underwear

V v

violin

volcano

vase

vulture

W  w

wagon

window

whale

wizard

windmill

walrus

wall

wigwam

X-ray

box

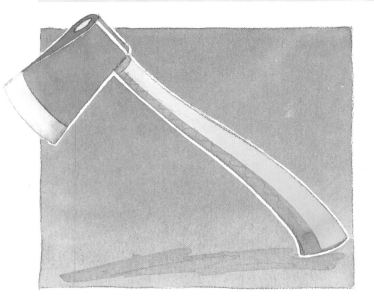

ax

fox

yacht

yo-yo

yogurt

yak

Z z

zebra

zipper   **zigzag**

Now see how many of these words you know:

INDEX

Aa
abacus
acrobat
alligator
anchor
ant
apple
arrow
avocado

Bb
balloon
bed
beetle
bicycle
boat
book
bubble
butterfly

Cc
cactus
cake
camel
camera
canoe
carrot
castle
computer
cow

Dd
daisy
dinosaur
dog
dolphin
donkey
door
duck

Ee
elephant
engine
envelope
escalator

Ff
fan
feather
fence
firework
fish
fork

Gg
garage
gate
goat
go-cart
goggles
gorilla
guitar

Hh
hamburger
hammer
hammock
helicopter
hen
hippopotamus
horse

Ii
igloo
iguana
ink
invitation

Jj
jacket
jack-in-the-box
jigsaw
jug
juggler

Kk
kangaroo
kennel
kettle
key
king
kite
kitten

Ll
ladder
ladybug
lamb
lasso
lighthouse
lion

Mm
medal
milk shake
mirror
monkey
motorbike
mouse
mug
mushroom

Nn

nail
necklace
needle
nest
net
newspaper
noodles

Oo

octopus
orange
ostrich
otter
ox

Pp

paintbox
pajamas
panda
parachute
parrot
penguin
piano
pie
pig
pineapple

Qq

queen
quilt

Rr

rabbit
radio
rainbow
raincoat
robot
rocket
rose

Ss

sand castle
sandwich
seal
seesaw
socks
submarine
sunflower

Tt

table
teapot
tee shirt
television
tent
tiger
tomato
tortoise
towel

Uu

umbrella
underwear
upstairs

Vv

vase
violin
volcano
vulture

Ww

wagon
wall
walrus
whale
wigwam
windmill
window
wizard

Xx

X-ray
ax
box
fox

Yy

yacht
yak
yogurt
yo-yo

Zz

zebra
zigzag
zipper